Mr. Shints

by
Sally Harball

DORRANCE PUBLISHING CO., INC.
PITTSBURGH, PENNSYLVANIA 15222

ISBN # 0-8059-5594-1
Printed in the United States of America

First Printing

For information or to order additional books, please write:
Dorrance Publishing Co., Inc.
643 Smithfield Street
Pittsburgh, Pennsylvania 15222
U.S.A.
1-800-788-7654
Or visit our web site and on-line catalog at
www.dorrancepublishing.com

Dedication

In memory of Chuck,
my loving husband and
best friend for fifty-two years.

Acknowledgments

I would like to thank so many friends who encouraged me to press on with my tenacious beliefs in this children's story. Special thanks go to my niece, Lauren Mills, and my son, Charlie, who provided the delightful likeness to Mr. Shints. Lastly, I would have given up without the support and patience of Chuck.

Author's Note

This story is a children's tale about a little girl, Amy, who discovers her conscience through the fantasy of her pet squirrel, whom she names Mr. Con Shints.

I find a very fine line drawn between morals and the Ten Commandments; between our consciences and our souls—all that busy business stashed between our ears; the stuff of which no other soul is cognizant. It's classified information in our private computer files, having arrived there by way of education, environment, experience, or, perhaps, all of the above. Whether or not we ever delve into this file is our unrivaled option.

Hasn't every child from four to one hundred and four had some form of a Mr. Shints in his or her life?

At the end of the story, I have provided reflections, questions for discussion, and some quotable quotes that pertain to each chapter.

Contents

❦ ONE ❧

Amy Meets Mr. Con Shints

"At last!" Amy sighed with relief. She hated the walk home from school. She just didn't like to walk, but this last part of her walk cast her into another world. She stopped at the bottom of what was called the *Shortcut,* put her lunch box on the ground, and took off her sweater. Tying the sweater around her waist, she was now ready for the climb. The shortcut was a very steep gravel path just off the city street. The path twisted like a snake, weaving its way through the woods and up to the street on the hill where she lived. Amy had to walk many city blocks on her way home from school, but she especially enjoyed this last little jog. The steep path through the woods was her private place away from cars, honking horns, screeching brakes, and all the other noises that go with busy city living.

Amy was in the second grade. Recently, in art class, she had learned how to make the color lavender, the same color as the flower. She had seen that flower in her Grandma's garden, and she loved the smell of her Grandma when she wore a powder called lavender. The fact is, lavender had become her favorite everything; the color, the smell of it, and even the feel of the word when it rolled off her tongue. She also was starting to call certain days her "lavender days." These days were absolutely the best days of all.

It was so quiet on this path without the street noises clanging in her ears. It was definitely a lavender day in Amy's mind. Bordering both sides of the steep path were many trees, bushes, and underbrush that harbored so much life. The woods seemed to quiver with activity, and each shadow and movement played with her imagination.

As she started her climb, many animals and birds chattered and sang to just her, she was sure. Amy was about halfway up the path when suddenly she heard a very loud tapping noise. It was so loud she could hear it over all the other friendly animal noises she heard every day. Probably a woodpecker, she told herself, but the tapping was so loud—more like a hammering noise. She just had to step off the path and go into the woods to see for herself.

Setting her lunch box down in the middle of the path, Amy gingerly tiptoed into the heavy underbrush. Green, feathery ferns brushed her legs as she made her way deeply into the woods in the direction of the hammering noise. Then she saw it . . . a huge bird, the size of a chicken, clinging to the trunk of a big fir tree. The bird looked like a chicken because the bright red feathers on top of its head looked like a rooster's comb. She had seen pictures of this bird in her mother's bird book and could even remember the name of it a . . . pileated woodpecker.

Amy was so excited, she turned and ran back out of the woods. She couldn't wait to tell her mother what she had seen. When she reached the shortcut again, she grabbed her lunch box and started running up the rest of the path. She hadn't gotten very far when she had a strange feeling that something was tugging at her, slowing her down, forcing her to stop . . . to think.

"I can't tell Mom I saw that woodpecker in the woods," she said to herself. "I'm not supposed to go into those woods alone, ever!" Amy knew about maybe getting lost in the woods or maybe even hurt, and no one would know where to find her.

She sat down in the middle of the path frantically trying to untangle her daydreaming from serious thinking. She just had to tell her mother what she had seen, but how could she do that without telling her she had been in the woods? Think think think.

"I know what I can say," she said, almost out loud. "I can tell her I saw that pileated woodpecker on a telephone pole on one of those city blocks I walk every day on my way home from school."

Just then, when Amy thought she had it all figured out, a very fat, gray squirrel scurried back and forth in front of her. Amy was sure that little squirrel was trying to get her attention. At least her imagination told her as much.

"Hello. Who are you?" she asked. The squirrel's big, bushy tail quivered with his every chatter while he fixed his gaze on Amy with his huge, black, marble-like eyes.

"They call me Conscience," said the fat little squirrel with another twitch of his handsome tail. "I'm your very own conscience, and I would like to be your friend. Everyone has a friend like me . . . a conscience."

Amy scratched her head. She was certainly puzzled. "I've never heard anyone say he or she had a squirrel friend named *Con Shints*," she said, pronouncing the words very slowly in an effort to figure out this strange name.

"Of course not," said the squirrel. "That's because a conscience will look different to different people. For instance, I look like a squirrel to you, but as your conscience, I'm always with you in your head, helping you learn the

3

difference between right and wrong. Not everyone pays attention though . . . such a pity."

"Well, Mr. Con Shints," she said, "I don't know if you make much sense, but I think I'll just call you plain Mr. Shints, even though it's the silliest name I have ever heard. So, Mr. Shints, if you would please get out of my way, I must hurry home to tell my mother about a pileated woodpecker I saw—on a telephone pole downtown," she added in a whisper.

"Wait a minute," called Mr. Shints. "Whispering doesn't make it right. Do you really think she's going to believe your made up story?"

Amy looked down at the little squirrel, her Mr. Shints. "Well, probably not," she said, "but I've been told again and again never to go into those woods alone. How can I tell her about that bird when I saw it in the woods where I'm not supposed to be?"

Mr. Shints stood up on his haunches in front of Amy. "You know what you must do, don't you," he said, with those shiny, marble eyes all but snapping at her.

Amy nodded. Actually, there were two things she knew she must do. First, she would never go into those woods alone again. Second, because of her newfound friend, Mr. Shints, she would not be able to lie by saying she saw that beautiful woodpecker on a telephone pole downtown. It would have to stay a secret that only Mr. Shints and she would ever know, locked up tight in her head forever.

Amy opened her lunch box and reached in for the bread crusts she often saved to toss into the brush for her special friends. "No wonder Mr. Shints is so fat," she thought as she placed the crusts on the ground in front of her. Fascinated, she watched as the little gray squirrel carefully picked up each piece of crust in his people-like hands and ate every one. Then he was off, back into the brush.

4

Amy closed her lunch box, got up, and finished her climb up the steep path that ended on the street where she lived.

"See you tomorrow, Mr. Shints," she called over her shoulder from the top of the shortcut. "I think I have known you before," she added, "but I'm not sure I've always listened to you. I'll try harder to listen from now on."

Lies

At a very early age, we all become acquainted with this scruple called a conscience. As the years pass, our consciences bump heads with numerous types of lies; some are called bold-faced, some are called white lies, and some are called mere stretches of the truth.

Do you know what a white lie is?

What kind of a lie do you think Amy was going to tell her mother?

Is there ever a good lie?

Do you think a white lie is a good lie?

Do you think Mr. Shints, your conscience, would warn you about lying?

❧ TWO ❧

About Instincts

Amy loved stopping halfway up the shortcut. It gave her an excuse to rest, but best of all, she could visit with her many magical friends in what she liked to call *her woods*.

When she reached the halfway mark up the steep path, she found her little squirrel, Mr. Shints, already out on the path, eager to see what kind of treat she had for him that day.

"I don't have my lunch box today, Mr. Shints," she told him, "but I didn't forget you."

With twitching glances, Mr. Shints took one peanut at a time from Amy's hand and stuffed them into his cheeks. He held the last one in his paws and nibbled around the edges until it was gone. Amy watched, fascinated by his method of eating.

"You sure know how to eat a nut, Mr. Shints. As a matter of fact, you are quite smart for just a squirrel."

"Just a squirrel," scolded Mr. Shints in his high-pitched chatter. "All squirrels have to be much more than 'just a squirrel' to survive in these woods. We have to be super smart," he told Amy. "Listen! Do you hear that?" The squirrel stood as if frozen.

Amy sat very still, listening to all the familiar sounds coming from her woods. Suddenly, she heard it, the same sound the squirrel had heard, the sound of a tinkling bell. Jumping up, Amy cried out, "Run, Mr. Shints! It's Queenie. You know how she would love to have you for a snack."

Mr. Shints had already disappeared when out of the woods, from the other side of the path, came a very large, very sedate, golden cat. A tiny silver bell hung from her bright blue collar. She pranced back and forth in front of Amy, and with her tail held high, she rubbed first one side, then her other side against Amy's legs.

Frowning, Amy asked the cat, "Queenie, just how many birds or squirrels have you eaten today?"

Queenie stopped her rubbing to look up at her. "How do you expect me to catch anything with this stupid bell hanging from my collar?" She stared up at Amy as if waiting for an answer.

"You're not supposed to catch anything," Amy scolded. "We feed you enough at home."

"Call it instinct, my dear," Queenie said with an irritating meow. "Haven't you heard of instinct?"

"Of course I have," said Amy, "but instinct means hunting for food when you are hungry. You can't be hungry with all the food we give you at home, you fat cat!"

"Instinct goes a lot further than hunger," meowed the cat. "It's instinct for we cats to stalk our prey. It's instinct to be alert at all times even when we are catnapping."

"Which is most of the time, you lazy cat," Amy scolded.

"We are just resting up for the instinctive hunt," said Queenie, once again rubbing her sleek body against Amy's legs.

"Instinct or not, you leave my friends in these woods alone," said Amy.

"A cat will be a cat," Queenie purred as she walked back into the woods from where she had come.

Instincts

I like to think of this phenomenon called instinct as another sense like the five with which we are familiar: sight, sound, taste, touch, and smell. Would instinct be a sixth sense?

Have you seen pictures of lions and tigers stalking their prey like Queenie? They have the instinct to hunt for food. Have you watched a dog, the ancestor to the wolf, shake a toy, toss it in the air, beat it against the ground, then lay on his *kill*, the toy, and take a nap?

How many animal instincts can you think of? Examples: hibernating bears, migrating birds.

Instinct—One of God's greatest accomplishments bestowed upon all living things.

❧ THREE ❧

Amy's
Healing Medicine

Amy was so deep in her private thoughts, as she climbed up the steep path of the shortcut she almost stepped on Mr. Shints. Her little squirrel was doing the craziest thing she had ever seen.

"Why are you rolling around on the ground like that, Mr. Shints? I almost tripped over you, and why all that noisy chatter? Whom are you scolding?"

"That's your whole problem, Amy," answered Mr. Shints. "You just don't know how to laugh, I mean really laugh. I wasn't scolding. I was laughing. In fact, I was laughing so hard, I just had to roll on the ground."

"Why were you laughing?" Amy asked.

"That's it in a nutshell, if you'll pardon the pun," said Mr. Shints in his merry little chatter. "You don't always have to have a reason. It just feels good. Try it. Let it take over your whole body. If you do it right, tears will run down your cheeks, tears that make you feel good, not bad. It will seem so silly, you will laugh even harder. Then you will feel so weak from laughing you will have to collapse on the ground and just roll around like you saw me doing."

Mr. Shints started up his little rolling act again. Amy giggled at her little friend. Then she laughed outright. The laughter came more and more until she was holding her sides. She just had to join her little squirrel now. She lay on her back, knees up in the air, laughing and laughing as tears streamed down her cheeks. Finally she and Mr. Shints fell silent.

"Didn't that belly laugh feel good?" asked Mr. Shints.

"Oh yes," said Amy. "Anything that makes you feel that good must be good medicine."

"Well, it is good medicine," stated the wise Mr. Shints. "So tell me, why such a glum face as you came trudging up the path?"

"You should know by now, Mr. Shints. Today is the day of my piano lesson."

"Ah, yes," sighed Mr. Shints, "the piano lesson."

"Now you're making fun of me," said Amy. "You just can't imagine how horrible it is. I'm supposed to memorize a whole page, and then Miss Mullet takes the page away and tells me to play it. I can't even remember one note. I freeze right up. I guess that's why I was looking so glum. I feel so bad about it all. I just can't do it!"

The squirrel stared back at Amy with his round, black eyes. "I think that bad feeling is called feeling sorry for yourself," he said. "Maybe if you can't think about anything else but feeling sorry for yourself, you'd do better by thinking of something funny."

"I know something funny," said Amy, suddenly in a brighter mood. "I'm positive Miss Mullet wears a wig. She's old, wrinkly, and bumpy. Without that wig, I bet her whole head looks like a big, wrinkly cantaloupe."

Both Amy and Mr. Shints started laughing, rolling on

the ground, giggling with delight over the thought of Miss Mullet's head looking like a cantaloupe. Finally, Amy got up and brushed off her clothing.

"I feel totally better, Mr. Shints," she said as she reached into her pocket for the squirrel's daily ration. As Mr. Shints took the peanuts from the palm of her hand, Amy said, "I bet when I get home I can play that whole page by heart, and at my next lesson, I'll do it there, too, or laugh trying, right Mr. Shints?"

As Mr. Shints chattered his way off into the underbrush, Amy knew he was still laughing . . . not scolding. Yes, it had turned out to be a laughing, lavender day after all.

Healing Medicine

What was Amy's healing medicine?

Does it feel good when you laugh?

Sometimes when things go badly for you, can you think of the funny side of it?

Give some examples.

"The world is a looking glass
and gives back to every man,
the reflection of his own face.
Frown at it and it will
in turn, look sourly upon you;
laugh at it, and it is a jolly companion."

Thackeray, from *Vanity Fair*

"Happiness can only be felt
if you don't set any conditions."

Arthur Rubenstein

❧ FOUR ❧

It's Not Fair

"It's just not fair, Mr. Shints," Amy whined, as she watched her little furry friend gingerly take peanuts from her hand.

"What's not fair, Amy?" he asked while his big, shiny, black eyes darted from one thing to another, always alert to any danger.

"It's everything most of the time," said Amy. "Take today, for instance. It was my turn to do the dishes with my nuisance of a little brother. He can't, or won't, do anything right, so I have to do most of the work. Then, to make matters worse, I have to go to bed at the same time he does. I'm treated like a baby. Sue and Phil get to stay up later because they are older, but I'm older than Timmy and still. It's just not fair. I get so mad at him sometimes."

Mr. Shints stood up on his hind legs to get a better look at Amy. He said, "I wonder if your big sister ever got mad at you before Timmy was born, when you were still the baby of the family."

"I don't know," said Amy. "We've always shared the same

15

bedroom, and she can sound pretty mad at me when I scream so loudly over my bad dreams. She would scream, too, if she had dreams like mine. What does she know anyway? She says she never dreams. How dull. I always dream, but that's a different matter, Mr. Shints. The fact is, I'm talking about Timmy. He is such a spoiled, rotten brat! I just hate him!"

Mr. Shints's big bushy tail began to twitch violently as he aimed his noisy chatter at Amy.

"Whoa there," he said. "Let's talk about that word *hate*. Look at the word, *hate,* as a big, sharp knife that can really hurt someone. Is that what you want, Amy?"

"Well, no, nothing like that," she said.

"So," said Mr. Shints. "What you really mean is that Timmy makes you so mad you could . . ." Mr. Shints stopped still. Then he said, "You could do this . . ." and he started to wiggle and jiggle. His little squirming body looked so ridiculous it made Amy laugh out loud, and she started to wiggle and jiggle with him.

Then, sitting very still, Mr. Shints said, "Maybe your sister thought you were a spoiled, rotten brat, too, but I'm sure she didn't hate you. Brothers and sisters don't always have to like everything about each other, and it's certainly understandable that they can get mad at one another, but HATE? Such a strong, hateful, word. Think of all the boys and girls who don't have a brother or sister with whom to play or even argue."

"Yes," said Amy. "I have some friends at school who have no brothers or sisters. They even like Timmy. They say I'm awfully lucky."

"You are lucky," said Mr. Shints. "Your brothers and sisters are the best friends you will ever have throughout your whole life."

"I guess you're right, Mr. Shints. I better go home now. It's almost Timmy's and my bedtime."

Hate

Do you think you could wiggle and jiggle, as Mr. Shints suggests, every time you get really mad at your brother or sister? It isn't easy, is it?

Can you think of a kind act you could do for your brother or sister that would replace that feeling of *hate*?

How would it make you feel if someone showed hatred toward you?

So often, hateful feelings come about through erroneous facts. The incident just wasn't what you thought. With a little effort to find the truth, perhaps followed by a wiggle and a jiggle, we might cure our hateful feelings toward our brothers and sisters. As Mr. Shints says, they are the best, lifelong friends we will ever have.

"Truth stands outside the doors
of our souls and knocks."

St. Gregory of Nyssa

ॐ FIVE ॐ

A Matter of Color

Amy sat in the middle of the path, dreamily staring into her woods.

"Aren't those trees pretty in all their different colored coats?" asked Mr. Shints as he busily filled his cheeks with bread crusts from Amy's lunch box. He stopped chewing to give Amy a long quizzical look. She seemed to be in a different world.

"I think something is on your mind, Amy. You're frowning," he said.

"Well, it's like this, Mr. Shints. Today at school, a friend taught me how to play that game with a little ball attached by a string to a paddle. He's really good. He can hit that ball a hundred times. We have a lot of fun, and we help each other with our school work, too."

"So why the frown?" asked Mr. Shints. "Sounds like you had a fun day."

"I usually do, Mr. Shints, but today, for some reason, girlfriends of mine started teasing me about him. They said I shouldn't play with him because he is dirty . . . dirty because his skin is darker than mine. Then, his friends started teasing him. They said he shouldn't play with me, that I am stupid because I am so pale. I just don't get it, Mr. Shints." Amy kept gazing into her woods that were all decked out in their colorful fall apparel.

"I think you do get it, Amy, and that's the reason for your frown," said Mr. Shints. "Don't you play with kids who wear different colored clothes?"

"Sure I do," said Amy.

"And don't you play with kids who have black or brown or red or blond hair?"

"Well of course I do. What's your point?"

"My point is, skin comes in different colors, too," said the wise Mr. Shints. "Let me explain. Look at that huge oak tree over there, wearing those brilliant red leaves, and look at that maple tree standing next to it, dressed in bright, golden leaves."

Amy's eyes jumped from one brilliant color to another. Swept up in the excitement, she said, "And there's a fir tree nearby that will wear its green needles all winter long. Oh, Mr. Shints, it's days like this, when I see all those pretty colors, that I know it has to be another lavender day."

"You bet!" said Mr. Shints. "And you know, Amy, all those trees need each other to bring out their own beauty. Their very difference brings out the best in each tree. All the different animals need each other, too," Mr. Shints added. "I know you have heard the racket the birds make when they see danger approaching. They are warning each other, but did you know they are also warning the rest of us in these woods? We all need each other, Amy, and we all become the best we can be by learning from one another and helping one another."

"How right you are, Mr. Shints. I need you, too, just like

you need me. At least you like my bread crusts."

Amy's frown had disappeared. Her Mr. Shints, given enough time, always came up with the right answers. She gently pushed her little friend back from her lunch box, snapped it shut, and walked up the rest of the steep path. Tomorrow she would see if her school friend would teach her how to hit that ball with the paddle, at least a hundred times.

Color

Prejudiced: A word meaning distorted, slanted, narrow mindedness—all describing what Amy was experiencing in elementary school.

What if we were all blind and could not see skin color or facial features? Do you think there would still be prejudice in the world? Isn't the color of our skin mere icing on the cake?

Do you think there is prejudice in your school?

What prejudices do you see in the country?

Louisiana De Crescendo said, *"We are all angels with only one wing; we can only fly while embracing one another."*

Amy's wise Mr. Shints said as much. If we would all just listen to our own Mr. Shints, what a better world it would be.

❧ SIX ❧

Sharing

"Achoo!"

Startled by Amy's loud sneeze, Mr. Shints jumped straight up in the air with all four legs and one bushy tail sticking straight out from his fat, little body. What a sight to behold! He was so busy filling his cheeks with his favorite treat, peanuts, that he really wasn't paying much attention to Amy who had been rambling on and on, something about roller-skating, but then she sneezed, and that got his immediate attention.

"You were saying?" questioned Mr. Shints, while trying to regain his composure.

"Achoo!" Amy sneezed again and then blew her already very red nose.

"Achoo isn't what I'm trying to say, Mr. Shints. It just so happens I have this terrible *code id by dose.* What I'm saying is about roller-skating. You remember, in the summer, when Mom let me walk all by myself to Jenny's house for her birthday party. It was a 'just girls' party, you know,

but then Jenny's mom said Timmy was out on the front sidewalk roller-skating back and forth, back and forth. Mr. Shints, he was begging to come in; that's what he was doing, just plain begging. Jenny's mom thought that was so cute, she invited him in for ice cream and cake. I was so mad at him, I—" Amy's last words caught in her throat, twisting her mouth into a mere hint of a smile. A slight twinkle showed in her eyes as she began to wiggle and jiggle.

"See, Mr. Shints? I just remembered what you said to do when I get so mad about something, and I was getting mad all over again." Then Amy stopped her wiggle and jiggle to say, "Ever since then, it's been kind of a joke in our house. We say that if you want something badly enough, you just roller skate back and forth, back and forth.

"So what's all this roller skating, begging business got to do with now?" asked Mr. Shints from a fair distance, should Amy let go with another sneeze.

"Oh, I don't know exactly," said Amy. "I was just thinking that roller-skating back and forth might sometimes get you what you want, like Timmy really wanted ice cream and cake. I do want a new bicycle so much, but I guess I'm not big enough for that just yet," she added wistfully.

"That's very wise thinking," said Mr. Shints.

"*Achoo!*" Amy sneezed again. "I also know that sharing takes care of a lot of wants in my life, so I don't really need to roller-skate to get them."

"For instance, like what?" asked Mr. Shints, his cheeks bulging with peanuts.

"Well," said Amy, "Sue sometimes lets me help her with her stamp collection if I'm real careful, and sometimes I let Timmy color a page in my . . . *Achoo!* . . . coloring book. Then he will let me color in his."

Wiping her sore little nose, Amy got up to leave. In a teasing chatter, Mr. Shints called after her, "And did Sue share that cold with you?"

"Yes she did!" said Amy, turning to stomp her foot in disgust. "I don't think that's what real sharing is all about, do you, Mr. Shints? *Achoo!*"

Sharing

Sharing—that's a tough expectation for little ones, but who said it was easy for *big* ones? When we were young, our siblings were the last ones with whom we wanted to share anything! But with our first real buddy, we swapped clothes, we swapped lunches, we swapped gum. You name it; that person was our buddy.

Can you think of times you were willing to share with your brother or sister or friend?

When you get older and busier in this *hurry-up* world, do you think you will be able to share of yourself with those who are less fortunate?

What kinds of things do you think you and your family could share? Example: Food Bank

Have you heard the saying: *"He ain't heavy—he's my brother?"* What does that mean to you?

✿ SEVEN ✿

Thank You

Sitting along the path, Amy shuffled around in her lunch box for the crusts she had saved for Mr. Shints. Her little squirrel sat patiently at her feet, his tail quivering with anticipation.

"Here you go, Mr. Shints," she said, carefully placing each piece of crust on the ground by her feet. The squirrel methodically picked up one piece at a time. He nibbled his way around each crust, never taking his eyes off Amy.

"I bet you are saying, 'Thank you,' with those big eyes of yours, aren't you, Mr. Shints?"

"That goes without saying, Amy, not 'thank you,' but the fact that you do say thank you often and always. Never forget to say thank you," said Mr. Shints, sitting quietly now, watching her. "What's all this thank you chatter about anyway, Amy?"

"Well," she said, "We've all been taught to say please and thank you, but for some reason, I've noticed it comes easier to some than others.

"Like—what do you mean, Amy?" asked Mr. Shints, still staring at her.

"I'll try to tell you what I mean, but it really confuses me. You see, I think it's really hard for boys to say thank you. Maybe they think it's sissy or something. I don't know. I just know my older brother, Phil, said the weirdest thing the other day."

"What did he say?" asked Mr. Shints, not paying much attention because he was busy scrounging for more crusts out of Amy's lunch box.

Amy went on with her puzzlement. "You see, Mr. Shints, our grandmother had given him a real cool radio for his birthday, something he really wanted, and Mom had been nagging him to write her a thank you note, but he just wouldn't do it. Why, I can't figure. Then, one day, after Mom nagged again, he got real mad back at her. He said, 'You make it sound like a barter, like there's strings attached. I'll give you something only if you thank me in return.' Now isn't that kind of a mixed up way of thinking, Mr. Shints?"

"Well, perhaps boys do come by a thank you harder than girls," said Mr. Shints, "but a thank you for something given is just plain, common courtesy in any language for any girl or boy, no matter what age."

"There's something else my brother doesn't seem to get," said Amy.

"What's that?" asked Mr. Shints.

"He doesn't realize that I was with Grandma the day she bought that radio, and it took her a lot of hours and effort to do the whole thing. She's not too young, you know."

"Ah, yes," said Mr. Shints. "Receiving a thank you can mean so much to a person, and a please is always nice to hear too. In fact, a please and a thank you can't help but put smiles on faces, giving people a truly lavender day, don't you think?"

27

"I totally agree," said Amy. Now, if you'll please get your nose out of my lunch box, I'll be on my way home."

Mr. Shints scurried off into the woods. Amy snapped shut her lunch box, and, with a smile on her face, she could be heard saying, "Thank you, Mr. Shints," as she hurried on home.

Thank You

We are all in such a hurry nowadays, so preoccupied with so many things—family, school, jobs, to name a few. It seems this thing called manners is fast becoming a lost art.

Have you ever noticed the smile on a person's face when you say please or thank you?

How many of you say, "Please pass the butter," at the dinner table?

How many of you say, "Thank you," when someone does something nice for you?

Please think about it. Thank you.

❧ EIGHT ❧

Amy's Heaven

Amy loved to snuggle against her grandpa's soft sweater as she sat on his lap listening to stories he read to her in his weak, scratchy voice. She had been told his voice sounded weak and scratchy because he was getting old. When her grandma would tell her it was time to get down from his lap, her grandpa would give her the tiniest smile. Amy liked to think of it as a *knowing smile,* as if she and Grandpa had a secret that only they knew about.

Then, one day, it happened. Her grandpa died. Amy had never known anyone who had died. She lay in her bed that night staring at the dark ceiling, unable to sleep. She was tormented with so many questions racing through her mind, such as where was her grandpa? At last she was able to smile at the dark ceiling, a smile of understanding . . . that *knowing smile* she and Grandpa had shared. Soon, she was asleep.

The next morning, Amy was in a hurry. Right after her breakfast, she grabbed a heel from a loaf of bread and ran out the door. Even in her hurry, she noticed how all the houses seemed to be still asleep as she ran across the street to the top of the *shortcut*. There, she sat on the bottom step at the top of the gravel path. While she quietly waited, she broke up the heel of bread into small pieces. Soon, after setting each piece on the step, she heard a rustling in the bushes. It was Mr. Shints. He peeked cautiously from under a fern, then came to the step where Amy was sitting.

"It's so sad that my old grandpa couldn't be new again," she said, while she watched the little squirrel pick and choose bread pieces, his whiskers shoving them about, "but I think I have it all figured out."

"What do you have all figured out?" Mr. Shints asked, through cheeks bulging with bread crusts.

"I think I know what happens when we die and go to Heaven."

Mr. Shints stopped chomping to look questioningly at Amy.

"Tell me what happens," he said.

"Well," said Amy, "When Grandpa gets to Heaven, he will find everyone he has ever known who has died right up there with him. Even Buddy, our old dog is there. The people who have died can be any age and size they want to be, and they can play with anyone they want. Grandpa can play with Buddy if he wants to. You see, they will all be new again, and someday, when I get to Heaven, I can play with Grandpa, too, because I will be new again, just like he is, like everyone is in Heaven. Every day will be a lavender day. Won't that be fun, Mr. Shints?"

"Yes, Amy," said Mr. Shints. "I think you have it all figured out pretty well, and, yes, that will be fun!"

Heaven

Tucked way back in our heads, we have all sorts of wisdom that has been passed down to us through the generations—wise prophecies about what happens when someone dies, but we haven't been there yet, have we? I found Amy's reflections on the subject very uplifting, didn't you?

> *"Heaven gives its glimpses only to those*
> *not in position to look too close."*

Robert Frost, from *A Passing Glimpse*

❧ NINE ❧

About Fire
and Listening

"Timmy, what are you doing?" asked Amy as she watched her little brother take a book of matches from a drawer.

"Come watch," said Timmy. "I'm going to do a magic trick."

"You better not be using matches," warned Amy.

"It will be safe," said Timmy. "Come on and I'll show you the trick over the toilet. If it doesn't work, I can drop the matches right into the water."

Amy couldn't resist seeing just what kind of trick her little brother was going to perform. She followed him into the bathroom. There, they kneeled down on either side of the toilet. Carefully, Timmy struck a match. He didn't strike it hard enough. He tried again. This time the match lit, but Timmy's fingers were too close to the heat of the flame.

"Ouch!" he hollered as the flame bit at his fingers. He threw the match, but it didn't land in the toilet bowl as he had planned. The burning match landed on the toilet seat.

Both Amy and Timmy watched in horror as the toilet seat suddenly began to burn. First black smoke, then hot, orange flames. Amy, quick to come to her senses, grabbed the bath mat that was draped on the tub and threw it over the toilet seat. The fire was gone, but the telltale signs lingered. The bathroom was full of stinking smoke from a charred toilet seat.

"Timmy, you're in big trouble," Amy scolded her brother. What Amy hadn't counted on was that her trouble was every bit as big as Timmy's.

She really wailed to Mr. Shints that evening as she sat on the steps at the top of her *shortcut,* handing out peanuts one at a time.

"It was all Timmy's fault! He started the fire, I didn't, Mr. Shints but Mom and Dad say I have to help Timmy buy a new toilet seat. It will take us months to pay for it from both our allowances!"

Mr. Shints stood up on his haunches to pluck another peanut out of Amy's hand.

"Don't you think you could have stopped Timmy from doing that trick, Amy?" he asked.

"I told him not to," she answered defensively.

"But then you joined him to watch the trick. You could have gone to your older brother or sister or anyone older in the house if he wouldn't stop for you."

"I suppose so," said Amy, hanging her head.

Sitting back to mull over his last peanut, Mr. Shints said, "Everyone makes mistakes, and this was a big one, Amy, but the trick is to learn from your mistakes so they won't happen again. You were lucky the whole house didn't go up in flames."

Amy let out a long, sorrowful sigh. "Mr. Shints," she said, getting up to leave, "I could really hear you in my head telling me all that stuff as I followed Timmy into the bathroom, but I just wasn't listening hard enough, was I?"

Fire and Listening

Fire is a powerful element that we've been taught to fear and revere.

Have you seen or heard about a terrifying fire?

Have you seen an awesome fire?

Have you ever had to call upon your own Mr. Shints when tempted with matches? Were you listening?

✒ TEN ✒

How Silly!

Mr. Shints darted out from the woods into the path. His bushy tail twitched with his excited chatter as he watched Amy climb the *shortcut* toward him.

"You just did the silliest thing, Amy," he chattered. "You just put the hood of your coat over your head now, when you are almost home. It is cold and windy. Why weren't you wearing your hood all the way home?"

"That's a silly question, Mr. Shints," she said. "You know Mom will be mad at me if she sees I'm not wearing it, but I just hate wearing that hood. None of my friends at school have a stupid hood attached to their coat. I feel so silly wearing it."

"None of your friends walk as far home from school as you do, Amy, or get earaches like you do," said Mr. Shints.

Amy drew circles in the gravel with the toe of her foot. "I know," she said, but it's not all that cold, and it's February already."

"Right," said Mr. Shints. "It is February, that month that

is squashed between the harsh jaws of January and the soggy mush of March; that month that would like to fool you into thinking it's not like January or March, but February is a hodgepodge of both, Amy. You have had the earaches to prove it."

"I know, I know," said Amy as she sat down along the path to open her lunch box for her wise little friend, "but I still feel so silly when I wear that hood."

"How silly!" scolded Mr. Shints.

"What's silly?" asked Amy.

"You, Silly, for feeling silly. Silly, silly, silly," he chanted as his shrill chatter became louder and louder and faster and faster until he was rolling on the ground, holding his fat little tummy with his paws.

It wasn't long until Amy was laughing too, as she merrily sang out, "Silly, silly, silly." When she finally finished her *silly* chant, she closed her lunch box and got up to leave.

"February will never catch me with another earache, Mr. Shints. Think of all the lavender days I will have without those earaches! It's only the *Sillies* running around with nothing on their heads, who will suffer from February's sneaky tricks.

Silly

Is what Amy was experiencing—not wanting to wear a hood because no one else did—what we call peer pressure?

What does peer pressure mean to you?

Do you like to dress like your friends?

If your friends were doing something you knew was wrong, would you be tempted to go along with it to be one of the gang, or would you let your Mr. Shints kick in?

❧ ELEVEN ❧

What Is Profanity?

Amy sat on the steps to the shortcut, elbows on her knees, chin in her hands, definitely scowling. Mr. Shints was busily working on his bread crusts, definitely ignoring her. Amy couldn't stand his ignoring her another minute.

"Mr. Shints, listen up!" she blurted.

Mr. Shints froze in his tracks. His paws, jaws, and tail, his whole body, in fact, stood like a statue. "I'm listening," he said, still not moving a muscle.

"Seems I'm always saying and doing the wrong thing at the wrong time," said Amy with such dejection that even the little squirrel looked as if he were starting to wilt.

"So what's the trouble, Amy?"

"Well, it's this thing called profanity. I always thought profanity meant words against God, but Mom has included in its meaning what she calls *toilet* words, or sounds out of place, even poor grammar."

"Wouldn't the world be a better place without those profanities, Amy?" asked Mr. Shints.

"I suppose you're right, but what doesn't seem fair is that Mom is charging us a penny every time she hears one of us slip up. I swear you can hear my penny clink in the jar more than anyone's. I'm going broke faster than my allowance cares to know about."

Mr. Shints stopped eating long enough to look up. "What are your biggest problem words, Amy?" he asked.

"One of them isn't even a word," whined Amy. "I burp when I shouldn't, like at the dinner table, but what really puts Mom on my case is when I say *'gotsto'* instead of 'have to.' I'm quickly running out of pennies!"

"I'll bet you'll have better grammar soon, Amy, and better manners, too, if your dwindling pile of pennies has anything to do with it."

"I bet you're right, Mr. Shints. I've sure been trying hard to squelch those burps at the dinner table. Well, I *gotsto* go now—oops! I mean I have to go now." Amy hurried off toward home while her little squirrel finished off the last of the bread crumbs and then ambled off into the underbrush.

Profanity

Do you know the meaning of profanity?

Do you know when you have used profanity?

Have you ever tried to make up your own silly word when you think a bad word might slip out?

Think of a silly word you could use when you spill something. For example, maybe words such as horsefeathers or fudgsicles would take the edge off.

❧ TWELVE ❧

Doctors, Hospitals, Shots, Oh My!

Amy was just plain "*ascared*." Her mother kept telling her she was either afraid or scared, not *ascared*. She was all of that. She had to go to the hospital to have her tonsils taken out. She knew this day was coming. All winter long, she had been miserable with colds, sore throats, and earaches, and her mother had taken her to the doctor more than once. Oh, those shots! But Amy was getting used to them and realized they weren't really so bad. It was the hospital that had her so frightened. Amy's mother had told her they would put her to sleep, and she wouldn't feel a thing, but still . . . what if? She didn't even know for sure what to *what if* about, and that was what she was so *ascared* about.

It was early summer now, and Amy had just completed her second grade in school. She loved school, and she had told all her friends that she was going to have her tonsils out. Somehow, telling them made her feel better since this adventure was going to be one her friends would want to hear about. Amy had been through all the necessary blood tests and shots. She was ready, she guessed. She had been told about the awful sore throat she would have when she woke up, but it wouldn't be sore for long. Yes, she was ready.

A few weeks later, on a warm July day, Amy rushed through the kitchen, grabbed a heel from a loaf of bread, and ran out the back door letting it slam behind her. She hadn't visited with her little squirrel in ages, and she wanted to tell him all about her operation.

Amy plunked herself down on the bottom step at the top of the shortcut. She called for Mr. Shints as she broke the heel of bread into small pieces. Her squirrel was at her feet in seconds, greedily snatching up the pieces as fast as she set them out on the step where she sat.

"Mr. Shints!" she scolded. "You're eating too fast. Don't you want to hear about my operation in the hospital? Well, I guess you can eat and listen at the same time, but that's *kinda* rude, you know."

Mr. Shints stopped chewing long enough to give Amy a quizzical look, but ever so briefly, so she told her tale anyway.

"It was like this, Mr. Shints. When I got into my hospital bed, they gave me a shot that didn't hurt a bit, but it made me so terribly sleepy, I couldn't have fun making my bed go up and down and bending it in all sorts of shapes. Then they put me on a cot with wheels on it and wheeled me into a big shiny room with bright lights. Because I was so sleepy, I can't remember too much, but I do remember them telling me to count backwards from ten. Isn't that silly? Well, I went right along with their silly game, but I can remember getting only to nine. I guess I must have fallen asleep. When I woke up, I was back in my room, still so sleepy, and so thirsty, and talk about a sore throat! They weren't kidding about that. I wanted a drink of water so badly but a nurse said I could only suck on ice cubes. Oh, Mr. Shints, the ice cubes felt so good on my throat, and then guess what? They brought me ice cream and Jell-O. I could eat as much of that as I wanted. It all felt so good on my throat, and the nurses were so nice, and my friends brought me lots of balloons."

Mr. Shints had finished all the pieces of the bread heel. Looking up at Amy, he said, "I'd say you had a fine time of it, Amy, and are now all set for a fun summer. When you start the third grade in the fall, you shouldn't be bothered with those blasted sore throats and earaches." With a flip of his big fluffy tail, the squirrel scurried off into the underbrush.

Amy called after him. "I did have a fine time of it, Mr. Shints. I found out there was nothing to be *ascared* about, or afraid of, or even scared. Fact is, you could almost call it fun . . . almost."

Doctors, Hospitals, Shots, Oh My!

Have you ever been to a hospital? Did you find it scary or almost fun, like Amy?

Did you know that hospitals often have clowns who go into the patients' rooms to make them laugh?

Do you think finding humor in a painful and scary situation might make it less painful and scary?

Helen Keller said, *"We cannot learn to be brave and patient if there were only joy in the world."*

Ah, yes, doctors, hospitals, and shots, oh my! Don't you think, besides being brave and patient, we must learn to laugh a lot?

❧ THIRTEEN ❧

Amy Is Lost at the Fair

It was the night before Amy's eighth birthday, and she couldn't sleep a wink. She was too excited. Her mother was taking her and five of her friends to the state fair. This outing was going to be the best lavender day of her whole life. At last, sunbeams burst through her bedroom window and splashed their golden rays all over her face. Her birthday was here.

When her mother parked her car at the fairgrounds, she told all the girls to hold hands to form a chain. Amy would be at the end of the chain, her mother at the front of the chain. In this fashion they paraded through crowds at the show barns, eager to see which animals won the purple ribbons, the best prize of all. Then it was time for the horse show and rodeo. The crowds swarmed to the entrances to the arena. In the push and shove of it all, the chain of hands snapped. Someone broke the hold Amy had with the girl next to her. Amy hollered, as did the girl whose hand she held, but no one was to hear as she floated free and alone as if she were in a sea of high waves. The waves of people were so high, she couldn't see where she was or where she was to go. She was spinning in circles.

Still unaware of what had happened, Amy's mother led the rest of the chain of girls through the crowds to their seats in the stands. Meanwhile, Amy continued to be bumped around by swarms of people until finally, there were none. She found herself all alone in one of the show barns. The only sounds came from the animals locked in their pens.

"Now what do I do?" she asked herself. "What would Mr. Shints tell me to do?"

"Snort!" came a sound from right under the gate where Amy had chosen to sit.

"Snort!" again, and this time, as Amy rolled onto her tummy toward the snort, she got a face full of sawdust. Wiping the sawdust away with the sleeve of her shirt, she found within inches of her face what looked like the biggest, pink button she had ever seen.

"That's not a button, that's my snout," said the mama pig who was lying on her side, nursing a dozen little, pink baby pigs.

"I know that's your snout," said Amy, "but it look likes a big button from here."

The pig asked in her snorty way, "Just what are you doing on your tummy anyway, nose to snout with me?"

"I think I'm lost," Amy said.

"You don't know if you are lost?" asked the pig.

"Of course I know if I'm lost," said Amy. "Well, actually," she added, "I know where I am. I'm lying here on my tummy, nose to snout with you. I just don't know where Mom and my friends are, that's all."

Amy could feel the tears filling up in her eyes. It was her birthday, and she wasn't supposed to cry on her birthday.

"I have a friend, Mr. Shints," she told the pig. "He usually tells me what to do when I am all mixed up, but I can't seem to get his attention, maybe because I'm too busy talking to you. You see, he's in my head someplace, but I usually do better when I can talk to him face to face. Oh, I'm so mixed up!"

"You're not mixed up," said the pig. "You are lost!"

Amy was having a very hard time with the tears that wanted to spill all over the place when, suddenly, she saw, right in front of her, a huge pair of cowboy boots.

"What have we here?" came a kind voice from way, way up. Amy's eyes followed the sound of the voice, up tall boots, up long, long legs, up past the official's badge on the shirt, and finally, up to a smiling face under a huge cowboy hat.

Suddenly she could hear her Mr. Shints loudly and clearly calling from some room way back in her head, "Never, never, talk to strangers. Scream and run if you are in trouble." Amy screamed. Her eyes darted back to the badge on the man's shirt. "Fairgrounds Guard," she read on the badge.

"I'm lost," Amy blurted.

"Well, let's just get you found," said the kind voice under the hat. He stooped and gently swung Amy up onto his shoulders. Up there, she could see everything! He carried her on his shoulders right to the announcer's box in the arena.

"Now, tell me your name and address, and I'll announce it to the whole world out there," he told her.

Amy leaned way over the top of his big cowboy hat, squashing it a bit so she could look him in the eye, even though she were upside down. She wanted him to get it right. Then, eye to upside down eye, she said, "My name is Amy Blair, and I live at 1736 North Maple Street."

Within minutes, her mom arrived at the announcer's

box to take her to their seats in the stands. Amy couldn't wait to tell her little squirrel how smart she had been; how she had listened to her very own Mr. Shints in her head and done the right thing.

Lost

Have you ever been lost?

What have you been told to do if you are ever lost?

Do you know your address and phone number?

✌ FOURTEEN ✌

Mr. Shints Will Play with Grandpa

Amy ran almost all the way home from school. She was so excited. As she ran up the steep path of the shortcut, she called for her pet squirrel. She wanted to tell him all about her first day of school in the third grade.

"Mr. Shints, I've got bread crusts for you." As she opened her lunch box, she called again. "Mr. Shints!"

"That's strange," she thought out loud. "He's usually here at my first call."

Then she heard it, feeble little squirrel chatter. She followed the sound to the edge of the path. Dropping her lunch box, she peered into the underbrush. There, she saw him, not two feet from where she stood. Her little squirrel was barely visible as he lay under a big fern next to a tree stump. Amy reached down to pick him up. Sitting at the edge of the path, almost afraid to even breathe, she gently put him on her lap.

"Oh, Mr. Shints," she gasped. "What happened? Did Queenie do this to you?" Amy was so frightened at the sight of her limp little squirrel.

"No, no, no," said the squirrel in a scratchy little chatter. "It's just . . . well, I've been awfully busy collecting food for the winter. Instinct you know. It's something I've done for many years, but I am getting old, Amy. As a matter of fact, I think this will be our last visit."

Tears spilled down Amy's cheeks as she rocked her little friend in the palm of her hand. He lay on his back, eyes closed now, and his handsome, bushy tail hung limply between her fingers.

"Oh, Mr. Shints, you sound the way Grandpa used to sound those last few days before he died. It's that same scratchy voice. Mr. Shints?" At the sound of Amy's voice, the little squirrel opened his round, black eyes to look up at her one last time.

"Mr. Shints, will you play with Grandpa?" Amy asked as she used the back of her other hand to swipe away a tear.

"Sure, I'll play with Grandpa," said Mr. Shints.

"Oh, but I don't want to lose you, Mr. Shints." Amy sniffed. "You're my best friend ever."

"You are only losing what you see here, Amy . . . the visible Mr. Shints . . . me, the squirrel. You may lose many visible friends throughout your life, but you will always have me as your invisible friend."

"My invisible friend?" questioned Amy. She knew, but she didn't want to hear it.

"You know, your Mr. Con Shints, silly, your conscience; the Mr. Shints who has told you so many wise things."

The little squirrel closed his eyes for the last time and lay very still. Amy sat quietly holding him in the palm of her hand. Suddenly, she was startled by rustling noises in the bushes next to her. She looked to see lots of gray squirrels peering at her. As she stood up, many black, shiny eyes watched her lean into the bushes as far as she could and tenderly set Mr. Shints under the fern where she had found him.

"Your family will take care of you now, Mr. Shints," she said.

Back on the path, she reached into her lunch box for the bread crusts she had saved for her pet squirrel. She carefully placed them along the edge of the woods. Then, looking up into the sky, a smile spread across her whole face. She was imagining Mr. Shints and Grandpa rolling around on one of those big, puffball clouds, laughing so hard that tears ran down their cheeks. They could do that, she knew, because they were both new again, not old with scratchy voices. A raindrop hit Amy on her face. She liked to think it was one of their tears of laughter that had seeped through their cloud.

Amy looked back to see many curious little squirrels sneaking out of the woods to test her bread crusts.

"Don't be sad, little ones," she said. "Your grandpa is already playing with my grandpa. You finish up those crusts now, and I'll bring you some more tomorrow."

The little squirrels chattered noisily as they worked over the crusts, holding each one in their paws just as Mr. Shints had done.

"I'll have to think up names for all of you, won't I? Just think of the many lavender days we will have!"

The rain was coming down quite hard now, so Amy ran up the rest of the shortcut. As the rain washed the tears from her face, she realized she was almost laughing with delight over her many new squirrel friends, but she was happiest of all in the company of her invisible friend, her conscience, whom she knew would be with her forever.

Grandpa Plays with Mr. Shints

As all the Amy's and their peers grow to adulthood, no doubt their Mr. Shints will remain intact, neatly tucked away within their souls to be called upon at their discretion. We will never understand all the happenstances we bump up against during our lifetimes, but, like Amy, with the help of our own Mr. Shints, we'll figure them out in our own way and time.

James Finley said, "To truly begin to figure out life is to accept its ultimately 'unfigure-out-able' nature that leaves us delightfully perplexed, humbled and grateful for a life we could not have planned if we tried."

Have you ever lost a pet? Do you dwell on this *unfigure-out-able* happening, or have you tried to turn it into Amy's kind of lavender day?

> *"Mystery on all sides!*
> *And faith the only star*
> *in this darkness and uncertainty."*

Henry Amelia